In this story ...

SUGAR - Hannah's toy fairy. Her skin changes colour, her magic dust can make you grow (or shrink) and she sings ALL THE TIME!

BLAZE - My toy dragon. He snorts fire and he can fly but he is a bit scared of pretty much everything.

HANNAH - I've tried to draw her name to show you what she's like. She jumps into things and has lots of feelings and stuff.

JO - That's me! I'm just me really. But every time we have a magical adventure with Sugar and Blaze, I'm the one who writes it down.

THIS is our latest adventure...

The Sugar and Blaze Adventures

Have you read them all?

That's Rubbish! ☐

Tinselpants! ☐

PRINCE
CHARM-BIN!

Jenny York

ILLUSTRATED BY LUKE COLLINS

For my Mum and Dad who have been in
love for over 60 years!

XXX

Find out more about
Jeny York by
visiting
www.jennyyork.com

First published in Great Britain in 2021 by Saltaire Books, Bradford,
England.

CHAPTER ONE

It was February.

Now I don't know what YOUR LIFE is like, but in MY LIFE February is dull and dark and rainy. You do get a week off school somewhere in the middle, but that's about all that happens.

This February though was about to get interesting.

And by "interesting" I mean bonkers and a tiny bit dangerous.

It all started one afternoon in school…

"OK, everyone," said Miss Green, "Who can tell me what **special day** is happening this week?"

Miss Green is awesome. She dreams up all sorts of **cool** lessons and this afternoon she had put craft stuff and glue on every table.

That was usually a good sign!

Miss Green pointed at my friend Sam, the only one with a hand in the air.

"Valentine's Day!" said Sam.

Every single boy in class looked disgusted. Most of the girls pulled faces too.

Love stuff.

Yuck!

"That's right," smiled Miss Green, **"Valentine's Day!** So this afternoon I'm going to show you how to make a **special card for someone you** love."

Miss Green winked.

Ben pretended to be sick on the floor. Luckily, Miss Green didn't see. She started snipping and glueing, showing us what to do.

I had to admit, when she was done it looked

pretty good!

The card was a heart-shaped man with springy arms reaching out to the sides. The arms made it look like the card wanted a hug.

"OK," said Miss Green, sticking her card to the board so that we could see what to do. "**Off you go!**"

In a flash the class became a chatty, busy mess.

"I guess I'll give mine to my Mum or something," said Sam. **"Who's your card for?"**

"Dunno," I shrugged.

But secretly, I did know. If I **had** to make

a love card, I'd be giving it to Blaze, my toy

dragon!

Now, before you start thinking **'That's silly, sending a card to a toy!'** there's something you should know.

When I got Blaze, my little sister Hannah got a toy fairy called Sugar. They were Christmas presents from my Grandma.

All sounds normal so far, right? But there's more!

No one else knew but these toys came to life...

...and that isn't all!

Sugar is covered in this magical dust stuff that can make Blaze grow to the size of a car.

Which means that I have a fire breathing, flying car!

And that comes in pretty useful, because since we got the toys WEiRd things seem to happen to us. These days we sort of attract magical trouble.

4

"Miss Green," said Ben, interrupting my thoughts. "I've finished the face on the front of the card. **Does it need a bum on the back?**"

People sniggered and Miss Green smiled too, rolling her eyes. She was used to Ben trying to make people laugh. (He's that sort of boy.)

"No, Ben!" she said, patiently. "**Your card does not need a bottom.** The back is where you write your love message."

As I coloured I started to wonder if my sister Hannah was making a card for her fairy, Sugar.

5

I hoped she was!

That crazy fairy would never stop singing about how sad she was if only Blaze got a card.

That's another important thing you should know about Sugar. She sings absolutely everything. Even simple things like 'yes' and 'no'. It drives Blaze mad!

"Right," said Miss Green. "Put your cards in your bags to take home. **Tidy-up time!**"

The class **WHIZZED** around putting things away.

At the front of class Miss Green unstuck her card from the board and tossed it into the bin.

I thought I heard an angry squeak as it dropped into the rubbish...

I thought I saw one of its happy hugging hands make a fist and give an angry little shake...

But at the time I figured it was just my overactive imagination.

CHAPTER TWO

At the end of the day, Hannah and Dad were waiting for me in the playground. Hannah was proudly waving a bright pink card covered in rainbow hearts and musical notes.

"Is that a card for Sugar?" I asked.

"Of course," said Hannah happily, *"Have you got one for Blaze?"*

I nodded.

"And what about me?" joked Dad, pretending to be sad. **"Where's my card?"**

Now, what you need to know about our Dad is that he's bonkers. And he's always talking some old nonsense. It's great!

"You'll probably get a card from Mum," I smiled.

"And a present, too?" asked Dad, hopefully. **"I know what I'd like for a present. I've always wanted a parrot. One that shoots lasers from its eyes!"**

"I think it's normally chocolates or flowers for a Valentine's Day gift," giggled Hannah.

"I'd rather have the parrot," grumbled

Dad.

"So at school today," said Hannah, ignoring him, "we learned about Saint Valentine,"

"Was he that **odd looking baby?**" grinned Dad. "The one who shot arrows to make people fall in *luuuuurve!*"

"No. That's Cupid," smiled Hannah. "But we learned about him too."

"Busy day!" said Dad. "So if he didn't shoot people with arrows what **did** Valentine do?"

"People aren't really sure," admitted Hannah. "He might have helped people get married... and he was definitely killed."

"Was it a parrot with laser eyes that killed him?" suggested Dad. **"They can be deadly."**

"No," giggled Hannah. "The point is, on Valentine's Day, you send a message to someone you love and write 'From Your Valentine'."

"I'm not doing that!" gasped Dad. **"What if your Mum thinks it's from someone else?"**

Hannah rolled her eyes.

"Then she might go looking for that person all over the world and get lost in a jungle and be eaten by a snake," he went on. **"This is dangerous stuff they're teaching you at school!"**

"Maybe just forget the card and get Mum a

present," I suggested, grinning.

"Or make a present!" he cried. "Let's make Hannah's **world famous chocolate brownie!** We could do it when we get home."

"I think that's the first sensible thing you've said in your entire life," said Hannah.

So, when we got home, that's what we did.

When it was bedtime, I couldn't wait to give my Valentine's Day card to Blaze.

Hannah and I share a room with a bunk bed. I sleep on the bottom and Hannah sleeps on the top. That's where Sugar and Blaze were waiting for us, still and lifeless, like any ordinary toys would be.

But as soon as Mum and Dad had said goodnight and disappeared downstairs...

RUSTLE RUSTLE RUSTLE

...our toys started coming to life!

"Sugar? Is that you?" Hannah whispered.

"Yes! Oh-Oh-Oh-yeah!" sang Sugar and

11

she flew up to the ceiling, her beautiful dress sparkling with fairy dust.

"Shhhhhhh," grumbled Blaze. "Mum and Dad will hear. You'll get the children in trouble!"

Sugar shot her sound blocking magic at the door.

"There!" she sang. **"Happy nooooow?"**

"I'd be even happier if you didn't sing," muttered Blaze.

"What?" she snapped.

"I said, 'I'm sure Mum and Dad won't hear a thing'," he said, giving Sugar a thumbs up and me a cheeky wink.

I think Sugar had heard though because her skin changed to an angry red colour. (Sugar's skin does that. It changes to lots of different colours depending on her mood at the time.)

Blaze pretended not to notice and turned quickly to me.

"Did you have a good day at school?" he asked.

Blaze loves to hear about school.

And, to be honest, I love telling him about it because he's always very impressed by how brave I am. He thinks stuff like learning cricket or answering questions in assembly sounds terrifying.

"School was great!" I said. "And look…"

I presented my heart card with a "Ta-da!".

Blaze was a blue dragon, but when he blushed it sent his cheeks a shade of purple. He was blushing now as he read my message.

"Thank you!" he whispered. "I love you too!"

Up on the top bunk, Sugar was shrieking with delight as she got her card.

"How wu-wuh-wu-wuh- wonderful," she sang.

She **WHIZZED** round the room, her skin glowing a happy yellow colour. Then I heard a musical **'Mwaaa'** noise up on the top bunk.

It sounded like Hannah was getting a rather dramatic kiss.

Not that surprising really. Everything Sugar does is dramatic!

Why? Ooooh why is the ketchup all gone? Gone! Oooh yeah gone!

"Oh gosh. You're tired!" worried Blaze suddenly, as I tried to hide a yawn.

"Maybe a bit," I admitted. "We should probably go to sleep."

Blaze nodded and snuggled down under my arm.

"I'll sing us all a niiiiiiiiice lullaby,"

offered Sugar. **"Something about LOVE I think, to celebrate Valentine's Day."**

"You don't have to!" muttered Blaze.

"Oh, but I'd like to," sang Sugar. **"No trouble at all. Now let me see. . ."**

"We need loooove, reeeeeeeal loooooooove"

Blaze shook his head in disgust and buried his ears deeper under my arm.

"To get us through the daaaaaaaaay!"

warbled Sugar.

Up on the top bunk, I heard Hannah give a contented sigh and, **in spite** of **Sugar's screeching singing about** love, we all drifted off to sleep.

15

CHAPTER THREE

The next morning, I noticed something STRANGE was happening the second I got to school.

Miss Green was humming to herself and almost dancing as she handed out the books.

"This morning we aren't going to finish our newspaper reports," she told us, smiling.

I guess in some classes that would be normal but trust me, in our class, that was REALLY WEIRD!

Miss Green loves doing things in order and she really loves getting things finished.

"What are we doing instead, Miss?" asked my friend Sam, frowning.

Miss Green beamed around the room.

"We are going to write poetry," she said. "Love poetry. **Now let's see…"**

She started to write on the board, singing as she wrote.

"Roses are red, Violets are blue…" She paused, tapping the pen against her lips thoughtfully. **"What rhymes with blue?"**

"Poo?" suggested Ben.

Everyone giggled, even Miss Green. She didn't roll her eyes at Ben like she usually did. Instead she scribbled it down on the board.

"**Poo! Yes!"** she cried excitedly. **"And zoo! That also rhymes with poo!"**

That lesson, Miss Green wrote down every silly thing Ben said!

And the more she wrote, the wilder things

got. Because once people realised that Ben wasn't getting into trouble, everyone joined in!

By break time my sides hurt from laughing, the board was covered in silly rhymes and we hadn't done a scrap of real work.

But Miss Green wasn't cross. In fact she looked delighted.

"Super-duper ideas!" she cried, clapping her hands together with glee.

"Shouldn't that be **'super-pooper ideas'**, Miss?" asked Ben with a snigger.

"Yes!" she agreed happily. **"Super-pooper ideas with smelly-jelly sprinkles on top!** This will make a perfect love poem for Mr Harding!"

Then, suddenly, she blushed **bright red** and shoo-ed us all out to play.

(In case you're wondering, Mr Harding is my sister Hannah's teacher.)

"Why does Miss Green want to write a love poem for Mr Harding?" I wondered aloud as we headed outside.

"I think Miss Green and Mr Harding are in **'super poo-per'** love," joked Sam giggling.

"Oh okay," I grinned. "That makes sense."

But the more I thought about it, the more uneasy I felt and the more I wanted to chat to Hannah.

I found her down by the tyres.

"Have you been writing poetry this morning?"I asked.

"Yep!" nodded Hannah. "Love poetry."

She was grinning. (I guess her class wrote super poo-per poems too.)

"Our poem is for your teacher, Mr Harding," I

told her. "Are your poems for Miss Green?"

"I don't know," shrugged Hannah. "We're finishing them after play instead of maths."

Instead of maths?

A wiggly worm of worry was starting to squirm around in my stomach.

"Hannah," I said quickly. "Sam thinks Miss Green and Mr Harding are in love."

"Oh, yes. They are!" agreed Hannah. "Everyone knows that!"

I figured she was probably right. Hannah was good at spotting that sort of thing.

"Look Hannah, just watch out, okay?" I warned. "I think SOMEthing WEIRD is happening again."

"Like what?" she frowned.

But at that moment the whistle blew and I didn't have chance to say any more.

I just had to hope she'd keep her eyes open!

CHAPTER FOUR

When my class had finished our *love poems* I volunteered to take them down to Mr Harding and luckily I got the job!

Mr Harding didn't look very impressed when I gave him our poems. (That wasn't a big shock. I was pretty sure they were 'poo-ey-zoo-ey' rambling rubbish!)

But what did shock me was what happened next.

"Well Jo," said Mr Harding with a smile. "**Since you're being St Valentine today**

and delivering all the *love notes*, you can **take our poems down to Mrs Broom!"**

MRS BROOM? THE HEADTEACHER?

Mr Harding walked briskly round the room gathering up the class poems.

"Please tell Mrs Broom that **I love her**, I mean, er, **give her my love**...I mean, er, **give her OUR love."**

Now Mr Harding was blushing!

That settled it! Something was definitely going on. There was NO WAY Mr Harding was in love with Mrs Broom. She must be at least 80 years old!

I shot Hannah a "DO SOMETHING!" look and she thrust her hand into the air.

"Mr Harding, please can I go with St Valentine to help?" she asked. "I could be Cupid."

"Yes! YES!" he cried, pushing us both out into the corridor. **"You be Cupid! Brilliant idea!"**

"You're right," whispered Hannah as we walked towards the office. "Something tricky is happening."

I nodded but before we could say any more we found Mrs Broom.

She was peeking into the school kitchen, **giggling**. I'd NEVER heard her giggle before. EVER!

"Erm, excuse me, Mrs Broom?" said Hannah, politely. "We brought some work to..."

Miss Broom spun round.

"**Yes! Yes! But SHHHHHHH!**" she said, snatching the papers from Hannah. "Can't you see I'm spying on Mr Piddlestix. **He's so** dreamy!"

Mr Piddlestix is the school cook. He makes an okay chocolate sponge but only a blind mole on a dark night would call him dreamy.

"**Ahhhhh, I do** love **Mr Piddlestix!**" sighed Mrs Broom.

Hannah's eyebrows shot up so high

23

that they nearly popped off the top of her head.

Because you see Mr Piddlestix was **grumpy**. He was **shouty**. He was the kind of **awful human** that on cabbage days would always put some on your plate **even if you didn't ask for any**.

TODAY:
CABBAGE STEW
CABBAGE PUDDING
CABBAGE JUICE

Why would Mrs Broom love a mean old stinker like that?

Meanwhile Mrs Broom had forgotten all about us and gone back to her spying. I peered past her into the kitchen.

Mr Piddlestix was sitting on the floor, surrounded by brussels sprout leaves.

"She loves me," he sighed dreamily, pulling off the leaves, one by one. "**She loves me not. She loves me. She loves me not! WHAT?"**

Mr Piddlestix sprang to his feet looking as mad as a toddler in a tantrum and hurled the sprout at the wall.

"She loves me NOT!" he cried, shaking his fists at the sky. **"Why? Why?"**

Just then, a SQUEAKY giggle echoed round the kitchen but before we could see where it came from Mrs Broom looked back at us and frowned.

"Back to class, you two!" she snapped.

So back to class we went.

But that wasn't the end of the Mr Piddlestix story. At lunchtime, he was out in the playground...

"I love you, you beauty!" he cried.

Then, he started kissing the leaves!

"Let's get married!" he suggested, hugging the bush even tighter.

Almost straight away Mrs Broom came striding across the playground wearing her serious face.

"Come along, Mr Piddlestix," she said crossly. **"You should be inside, dishing out the dinners."**

She pulled him back towards the hall but Mr Piddlestix kept blowing kisses at the bush.

"I love you," he shouted one last time, as Mrs Broom yanked him inside. **"CALL ME!"**

Then, I heard it again! A SQUEAKY giggle coming from inside the bush.

Obviously, I went to check it out but there was nothing there. I figured I'd check again at home-time just in case.

But unfortunately, when Dad came to pick us up at home time, Mrs Broom was chopping the bush down!

"Why does he love a bush…" she grumbled as she hacked at the branches. **"…when he could love me!"**

She almost screamed that last bit and a passing parent jumped in alarm.

"Pardon?" asked the mum, looking worried.

Mrs Broom suddenly realised a lot of children and parents had stopped to stare at her.

"Oh, I was just saying 'Why have a bush when you could plant a tree!'" she said sweetly. **"I just 𝓁ℴ𝓋ℯ trees!"**

And then, desperate to prove her point, she darted over to a nearby tree and gave it a hug.

"Protecting the planet!" called Dad with a cheery thumbs up. **"Great job!"**

But as we walked away, he frowned.

"Tackling climate change by chopping stuff down?" he muttered under his breath. "I think Mrs Broom needs a holiday!" ★

Hannah gave me a meaningful look.

We needed to talk to Sugar and Blaze.

★ Important note: Always be kind to your teachers, even and perhaps especially the bonkers ones. My Mum's a teacher and believe me they often just REALLY NEED A HOLIDAY!

CHAPTER FIVE

Sugar and Blaze agreed that something WEiRd *was* going on, so the next morning we smuggled the toys to school to check it out.

"Just don't let anyone see you!" I warned.

"Well obviouslyyyy!" sang Sugar but Blaze just nodded, his eyes wide.

He was glancing around nervously, like he expected an assembly to pounce on him at any second.

As soon as Hannah and I went into class the toys flew off to see what they could find out. I kept an eye on the door to the corridor and in no time at all they were back.

I pretended to need the toilet and ducked out into the corridor to see what was happening. Hannah was already out there. And she seemed to be panicking about crayons.

"I tried to draw something blue and it came out pink," said Hannah. "Then I tried the green and it came out pink. Every colour came out pink!"

"Yikes!" said Blaze.

"**Crayons are the least of our worries**," sang Sugar. "**Come and see!**"

"But won't we get into trouble?" I asked.

"**There's so much magic in the air right now that Blaze could dance about with his pants on his head and no one would notice.**" she sang.

"Sugar! Really!" said Blaze blushing purple at the thought. "You know very well dragons don't wear pants!"

"**Just come oooooooon!**" she sang.

We ran through the school to Mrs Broom's office and Sugar pushed open the door.

"Come in," said Mrs Broom, in a dreamy sort of voice. "Isn't it a lovely day to be in love!"

Before we could reply Mrs Broom sneezed loudly ...and pink rose petals shot from her nose!

Hannah gasped, but Mrs Broom didn't seem

bothered at all.

"I *love* rose petals!" she said. "So romantic!"

"More like, sooooooooooo snotty," sang Sugar in a cheeky whisper.

Sugar and Hannah started to giggle.

"Achoooo!" sneezed Mrs Broom again, spraying more petals. "Achooo! Achoooo! Achooo!"

"Wait!" joked Sugar. **"I think she's singing the end of 'When Santa got stuck up the chimney'."**

Hannah and Sugar were both in hysterics at that.

"We should sing too!" suggested Sugar cheekily. **"Achoo! Achoo! Achoo!"**

"Sugar! this is serious," groaned Blaze.

"Achoo! Achoo! Achoo!" sneezed Mrs Broom.

"Achoo! Achoo! Achoo!" echoed Sugar. **"All together now . . . Wheeeeeeeeeeen**

Santa got stuck up the chimney. . ."

Hannah hugging her sides and laughing so much now that she couldn't catch her breath.

"Let's just go," I suggested. "I think we've seen enough."

But then...

"Hee! Hee! Heee!" squeaked a delighted voice. "Heeeeee. He he he heeeeeee!"

Peeking from the bookshelf was a pink paper heart with bendy arms and a wicked grin.

Sugar stopped laughing at once.

"Time to go!" she yelped and wafted us out of the room.

Out on the corridor Blaze looked terrified.

"D-d-d-did you see that?" he stammered **"That was the card you made for me!"**

"No," I said, realising. "Your card's at home. I bet that's the card Miss Green made. She threw hers in the bin."

"Well it's not in the biiiiiin any

more!" sang Sugar grimly.

"**Hide,**" hissed Hannah. "**It's coming out!**"

We ducked behind a bookcase, just in the nick of time.

The Heart-Card-Man came bouncing out of the office, waving his bendy arms in the air with glee.

"**Petal bogies!** It's <u>**SNOT**</u> going well for Mrs Broom!" he giggled. "Time to check on my other little project...**the farty party!**"

And with that, he was off!

He was surprisingly fast for such a little card and in seconds he had bounced right across the hall and into the school kitchen.

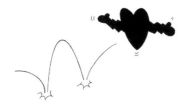

"**After him!**" cried Hannah.

We all dashed to the kitchen door and peeked

inside, but Heart-Card-Man had vanished.

"He must be hiding in a pan or something," whispered Hannah. "What do we do now?"

"Oh n-n-no!" wobbled Blaze, pointing. "Look!"

Mr Piddlestix was making trays and trays of chocolate.

There was no dinner in sight!

"**Something tells me you won't get your 5-a-day todaaaaay**," joked Sugar.

But that wasn't the worst of it!

Suddenly, Mr Piddlestix made a loud farting noise and **SHOT** into the air in a cloud of petals.

When he landed again, he was giggling and holding a bunch of red roses.

"Oh my goodness!" gasped Hannah. "Did Mr Piddlestix just fart roses?"

Sugar exploded with laughter so of course Mr Piddlestix spotted us (great work Sugar!) and called us into the kitchen.

"Come in! Come in!" he said dreamily. "I'm in *love* with a bush and I fart roses."

That was the final straw for Sugar and Hannah. They both just collapsed in fits of giggles.

"Erm… That's nice!" I said, trying my best to be polite.

"Is it?" he giggled. "I thought it might be a bit of a problem. Because I fart a lot. What shall I do with all the roses?"

"Well, definitely don't give them as a gift," spluttered Hannah, between giggles. "That's really not hygienic."

Sugar screeched with laughter but Mr Piddlestix didn't seem to have heard properly.

"Give them as a gift!" he cried. "That's an excellent idea!"

"No, wait!" I yelled.

But it was too late.

Mr Piddlestix had snatched up all his fart roses and he was running for the door.

CHAPTER SIX

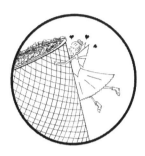

There had to be a way to stop him!

Hannah was crying with laughter and Blaze was flapping to and fro in a bit of a panic. But Sugar was just watching in delight. And SHE was between Mr Piddlestix and the door.

"Sugar, do something!" I cried.

"**On it!**" she sang merrily.

In a flash she snatched up an enormous pan and clunked Mr Piddlestix round the head.

He froze.

His eyes crossed and a big silly smile slid onto his face.

"Have some more cabbage," he

slurred.

And then he dropped flat on his face into an enormous pile of his own fart petals.

"Sugar!" gasped Blaze. "What have you done?"

"Jo said 'DO SOMETHING'," grinned Sugar. "So I did something."

"She meant something magical," he snapped.

Sugar shrugged.

"Then she should have been more specifiiiiic," she sang with a cheeky grin.

Mr Piddlestix gave a deep sigh and snuggled down into the petals like an ugly, sleeping baby.

"Looks like he'll be okay," said Blaze peering at him. "Just..."

But at that moment the kitchen door swung open again. Looking over, we saw a flash of pink leaving the kitchen.

"The card!" hissed Hannah pointing. "Come on!"

We reached the door, just in time to see Heart-Card-Man bouncing into the staff room and we all **SPRINTED** after him.

But at the door I hesitated. Kids weren't allowed in the staff room. Hannah, however, didn't seem to care. She pulled me straight inside and we dived down behind a settee to hide.

"Now what?" whimpered Blaze.

Hannah bobbed up like a meerkat with a death wish, to see what was happening.

"Hannah! Careful!" I hissed.

She dropped back down beside me.

"No teachers," she whispered. "The card's on the photocopier!"

"The photocopier?" I frowned. "What's he copying?"

"Himself!" she admitted, looking grim.

At that moment Heart-Card-Man giggled his horrible, squeaky laugh.

"Soon, I'll have an army of cards to do my evil work," he cried. "Millions of people will fall in love..."

He chuckled darkly.

"...with people who won't love them back," he paused. "Or things that can't love them back...like trees, toilets, tins of beans. Heeeeee heeeee heeeeeeee!"

Hannah gasped.

"Like poor Mr Piddlestix, in love with that bush!" she hissed.

I nodded. I'd heard a fair few evil plans in my time but **this was a real stinker**.

"Then they'll know what it's like," said the card his voice wobbling. "To be tossed aside...to be thrown into a bin."

And with that, the door slammed with a

For a second no-one moved or even breathed, but then Hannah peeked up to check the room.

"**He's gone!**" she announced, standing up fully. "**Looks like you were right, Jo!**"

I nodded glumly.

"**He's definitely the card Miss Green threw in the bin!**" I agreed.

"**Hmmmmm. THE BIN,**" echoed Sugar thoughtfully.

But she wasn't singing. And her skin had

turned a bright neon pink. Suddenly, she started walking across the room towards the photocopier.

"That bin," sang Sugar, dreamily pointing. **"I've never seeeeeeen such a handsome biiiiiiiin. He's like the Prince Charming of all bins."**

She scooped the bin by the photocopier into a tight hug. Then she dragged it over to where we we were standing.

"Hey everyone!" sang Sugar, panting slightly with the weight of the bin. **"This is my new boyfriend, Prince Charm-Bin."**

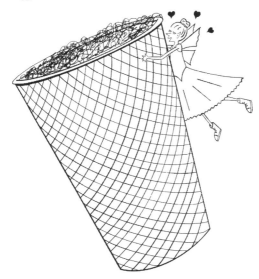

"Oh boy! This is bad," worried Blaze covering his face with his claws and shaking his head. **"Very, very bad!"**

"What's happening?" I frowned. "I figured the card's love magic was only messing with the grown ups. All the kids in my class were still fine."

"And we're still fine," added Hannah.

We all peered at Sugar and her new boyfriend, trying to puzzle it out. Sugar just smiled serenely.

"I think..." said Blaze cautiously, "...that maybe you have to **want** to fall in love for the magic to work properly."

"So anyone who thinks all that mushy stuff is a big pile of yuck?" I asked.

"They should be fine!" finished Blaze nodding. "But poor old Sugar, who <u>likes</u> that love stuff."

Hannah looked like a volcano about to erupt.

"I'm going to find that stupid bit of card and tear it up!" she said, eyes blazing.

"No!" said Blaze, looking alarmed. "What if I'm wrong? What if we all end up **hugging**

44

bins or **in love with hoovers** or...or..."

"**Smoooooching with spoooooons**," suggested Sugar dreamily.

"Exactly!" agreed Blaze.

"Then what do we do?" asked Hannah.

Blaze took a deep breath and stood up a little straighter.

"We go for help," he said, looking terrified but determined. "Sugar, do your thing! **Dust me!**"

"**What?**" she sang, looking up from her bin cuddle in surprise. "**Oh....dust. Right!**"

She flew above Blaze, spinning and shaking her skirt until he was covered in the sparkling, magical fairy dust.

Immediately, Blaze started to grow. He **BLASTED** out of a fire door and we **DASHED** after him. Out in the playground he grew and grew until he was as big as a car.

"Hop on!" he smiled.

"**Can I bring Prince Charm-Bin?**" sang Sugar dreamily.

Blaze rolled his eyes.

"Sure. Why not?" he grumbled.

We all clambered onto Blaze's back and he **SHOT UP** into the sky, until we were high above the clouds.

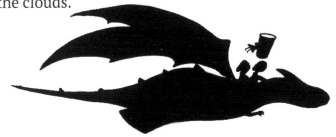

"So, where are we going?" I shouted as we **WHIZZED** through the icy wind. "Who can possibly help with this kind of mess?"

"St Valentine," Blaze shouted back. **"He's a big fan of cards and messages** but he doesn't like **real** visitors. He'll be well guarded."

"We can do it!" shouted Hannah.

"I luuuuuuuuuurve you, Prince Charm-Bin!" sang Sugar, which was less helpful.

"Nearly there!" called Blaze.

The clouds were changing colour. Pretty soon they were as pink as Sugar's skin. Blaze gave a satisfied snort of fire and began to spiral down.

"So, where exactly does Valentine live?" called Hannah, peering into the mist.

"The Land of Love," yelled Blaze. **"Hang on!"**

And with a final swoop he landed with a bump in a large orchard.

Hannah and I slid down to the ground. Sugar followed, still cuddling her bin-friend... boy-friend... whatever!

"**Those treeeeees are covered in chocolates**," sang Sugar dreamily, pointing at a nearby branch.

"Crikey, she's right!" gasped Hannah in delight.

Her fingers began reaching for one of the delicious treats but...

"No! Don't!" I said pulling her hand back. "It might not be safe."

"OH, IT'S DEFINITELY NOT SAFE," growled a menacing voice.

CHAPTER SEVEN

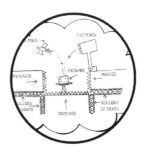

walking towards us was a grumpy looking baby.

He was wearing a nappy- **just a nappy**- and carrying a golden bow and arrow.

And he had white fluffy wings! **(I probably should have mentioned that first.)**

"You're Cupid?" guessed Hannah.

The little baby nodded, scowling.

"Yes. And I'm also Head of Loveland Security! Nobody goes through this orchard. And nobody touches the chocolate," he ordered. **"It's not allowed."**

He might have looked like a baby, but he had the head of a grumpy old man, which made me want to giggle. I was sure Sugar <u>would</u> giggle, but luckily she was still too busy hugging her bin. **"We need to see St Valentine,"** explained Hannah, stepping forward. **"It's important."**

"Well," Cupid sniffed and drew himself up to his full baby height. **"Mr Valentine does not wish to be seen!"**

At that moment, a flock of white doves fluttered into the orchard, landing softly in one of the trees.

"Doves! How romantic. I... aaaaargh aaaaaaaargh," wailed Sugar as Cupid barged past, knocking her flying.

"GET AWAY FROM MY CHOCOLATES, you 'orrible pests!" roared Cupid.

He charged into the air, swiping at the birds with his bow and aiming some nasty flying kicks in their direction. But the doves were too quick for him. They just fluttered away. In fact, their cooing sounded suspiciously like giggling.

Cupid came back to the ground with a thump, looking grumpier than ever.

"That wasn't very kind," scolded Hannah. "Why are you being so mean to those poor sweet doves?"

"POOR SWEET DOVES!" snorted Cupid. **"Those 'orrible pests steal my chocolates. I'm forever shooing them away. Can't remember the last time I got to drink a full cup of tea in peace."**

"Oh, I see," said Hannah, frowning. "That's rubbish."

"Rubbish!" agreed a nearby caterpillar, before remembering he was from a different Sugar and Blaze story.

"It **is** rubbish," agreed Cupid, nodding his angry baby head. **"I've tried shooting them with my arrows but look!"**

And before any of us could object he shot a golden arrow and **blasted one of the doves!**

There was an explosion of glitter but when the sparkly dust settled, the dove was still there looking dazed and dreamy. (Don't ask me how a dove looked dreamy. It just did!)

"SEE!" Cupid screamed. **"It just makes them fall in LOVE."**

"I'm in love-love-love," sang Sugar, **"with this handsome bin-binny-bin-bin, oh yeah!"**

Cupid frowned in confusion.

"The singing fairy's in love... with a bin?" he asked slowly.

"Yes," nodded Hannah. "And that's actually not the worst of it."

"We **really** need to see Valentine," I pleaded. "If we could just ..."

Cupid shook his head.

"Nope! Look, clearly you've got problems," he nodded towards Sugar. "But I can't let you past. I've got enough problems of my own."

Now that was a fair point, but I wasn't about to give up!

"What if we fixed your dove problem?" I suggested. "Then could we go past?"

He shrugged.

"Maybe."

"Okay then...!" I said, thinking. "What if we attract the birds to something else instead. Like Hannah's brownie, that's yummy and chocolaty. I'm sure that would work."

For a second, Cupid looked almost happy. He

did a little dance of excitement.

"LIKE A TRAP?" he grinned, an evil look in his
baby eyes.

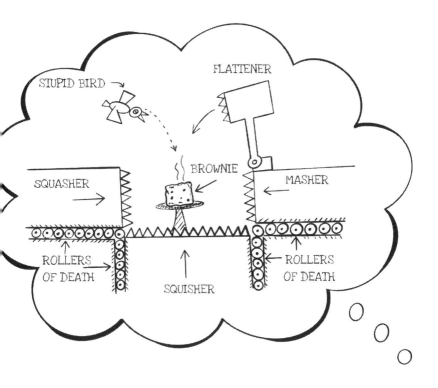

"More like a distraction," I said firmly. "You
can't use my ideas to hurt the birds."

"Fine," scowled Cupid, immediately back to his
grumpy self. **"Give me this 'amazing brownie' and if**

it works I might 'accidentally' let you past."

Hannah gave me a joyful thumbs up but Blaze was biting his lip.

"Jo, I always love your ideas," he whispered. "But we don't really have <u>time</u> to bake brownie."

"And WHY is that EXACTLY?" snapped Cupid glaring in his direction.

"Well, erm, we have to get some help from Valentine and, er, save the day," said Blaze, shuffling from foot to foot with nerves.

"That's true!" sang Sugar, looking up from her bin. **"And I need to get back home soon because I'm getting married later today . . . to Prince Charm-Bin!"**

Cupid opened his mouth like he wanted to say something but then closed it again with a frown.

"What if I just gave you the recipe, Cupid" suggested Hannah, getting us all back to the point.

"I suppose that'll have to do," grumbled Cupid.

He magically produced a pad and pen from thin air and passed them to Hannah who started to scribble. When she was done she pressed it into Cupid's pudgy hand.

Cupid looked down at the note, then back to Hannah, considering.

"Go on then!" he grumbled eventually. **"I'll pretend I didn't see you. But this brownie plan had better work!"**

"Oh, thank you!" cried Hannah scooping

him into a hug.

"**Gerroff!**" he complained, wriggling away. "**Valentine's house is that way...over the hill...just past the petal monster.**"

"The WHAT?" spluttered Blaze. "Did you just say 'petal monster'?"

But Cupid was already flying away to bake his brownie.

"Come on," said Hannah grimly. "We have to keep going. No matter what!"

As we climbed the hill, Sugar started shaking her head and rubbing her eyes. Her skin was turning back to the normal purple colour.

"Sugar!" cried Hannah. "Are you feeling better?"

Hannah turned to me in excitement.

"Maybe the card's love magic is wearing off now we're so far away from it," she said hopefully.

"Maybe," I agreed.

Sugar was blinking now and looking at her

precious Prince Charm-Bin in confusion. Then…

"**Urghhh!**" she shrieked suddenly. "**Why-why-why am I hugging a bin? Disgustiiiiiiiiiiiiiiing!**"

A mighty roar bellowed around us.

"**I'M DISGUSTING NOW AM I?**" growled an angry voice. "**ON TOP OF EVERYTHING ELSE!**"

Blaze gulped.

"Oh boy," he squeaked. "That'll be the monster."

CHAPTER 8

Suddenly, the air filled with pink petals, smashing against us in gusts of confetti.

"FEAR ME!" roared the voice. **"RUN FROM ME!"**

"It's down there!" cried Hannah swatting petals away from her head. *"Come on!"*

And off she went **DASHING** TOWARDS the danger. **Typical Hannah**.

We **RUSHED** after her, leaning into the flowery hurricane that was pushing us back. The petal wind got stronger. It started to lift us off the ground, whirling us round until...

It   dropped   us....right   at   the   feet   of   a

MONSTER.

Towering over us, as big as a house, was a pink, petally bear.

"I SAID 'RUN FROM ME!'" it roared, showering us with more petals. **Don't you people listen?! Seriously, this is the WORST DAY EVER!"**

And then, with a scream of frustration, the monster sank to the floor and began to sob into its petally paws.

Hannah tiptoed closer. (I know. She's crazy!)

"Erm...Hi" she whispered gently. "I'm Hannah. What's your name?"

The monster looked up. It had long pretty eyelashes that were sparkling with tears.

"Well, my name is Perilous, Enormous, Terror-At-Large the

3rd," she explained, **"But you can call me Petal."**

"Petal," smiled Hannah. "That's a lovely name."

The petal-bear-thing smiled back.

"Oh, thank you," she sniffed wiping her eyes and getting back to her feet. **Now if you don't mind, I just need to petal smash you to bits."**

Petal raised a flowery fist above Hannah's head.

"Wait!" cried Hannah. "No smashing! We don't want any trouble. We just need to see Valentine."

Petal frowned in confusion.

"BUT Mr Valentine doesn't like visitors. He only likes letters and

songs and . . . Oh what am I going to do?"

She started wringing her hands with worry causing showers of confetti.

It was like being at a **very dangerous** wedding.

"Oh, please tell us what's the matter," Hannah begged. "Maybe we can help."

Petal shook her head sadly, causing more petal showers.

"I need to write a love song for Mr Valentine." she said. I write one every year to celebrate Valentine's Day."

"So, what's the problem?" frowned Hannah.

"This year I can't think of one," she whimpered.

"Well, I'm sure he'll understand," said Hannah soothingly.

Petal glared at her.

"HE WON'T," she snapped. **"Last time I messed up he made me fall in love WITH A CARROT."**

It was magical

I expected Sugar to giggle but instead she looked cross. Maybe she was remembering the whole bin-friend boyfriend thing.

"I'll help you!" sang Sugar. **"You see, I'm a bit of a song writer myself, la la la laaaaaaaaaaaaaaaaaaa."**

Blaze pulled a face and covered his ears but

Petal looked hopeful.

"Are you any good?" she asked.

"Any good? Any go-oo-oo-oo-ood?" Sugar sang. **"I'm faaaaaaaaaaaaaaa-bu-lous!"**

Sugar winked at Hannah and started to sing.

"We need love...

Love! Love!

...to brighten up the day.

Reeeeeeal love...

LOVE! LOVE!

...to make things feel OK.

All we need is true love

and maybe chocolate

brown-aaaaaaaaay!"

"Amazing!" cried Petal. **"And so catchy...reeeeeeeal love..."**

Sugar turned her happiest bright yellow colour and gave a theatrical bow.

"Oh this song is going to be a big hit, I just know it." said Petal dancing away in a cloud of petals and humming Sugar's song as she went.

"Let's sneak past," hissed Sugar, **"while she's distracted."**

"But she didn't exactly say we could go past," whispered Blaze. "What if..."

"Oh don't be such a worry pants!" sang Sugar **WHIZZING** forward. **"It'll be fine."**

We set off again and soon the path led us into a dark dark wood.

Now, you're a smart kid so I'm guessing you know what dark woods can be like.

To be honest, we've had some bad experiences with dark woods ourselves in the past so I wasn't massively surprised when…

"MA-RRY-ME!" growled a voice.

"Did someone say 'Marry peas'?" asked Sugar, looking puzzled. **"No, that doesn't make sense. It must have been 'mushy peas'. I wouldn't mind some mushy peas! Have we had any lunch today?"**

"MA-RRY-ME! MA-RRY-ME! MA-RRY-ME! MA-RRY-ME!"

Somewhere in the dark trees hundreds of voices started chanting the same message, over and over, like a drum beat.

"MA-RRY-ME! MA-RRY-ME!"

Then they came shuffling out of the greenery in a swirl of pink mist. An army… of teddies!

Each one was staring forward blindly and clutching a fluffy heart. And on each heart it said,

you guessed it,

"MA-RRY-ME!"

Now that the bears had popped out from their hiding places, they had frozen. In fact they could have been ordinary teddies except for the

"MA-RRY-ME! MA-RRY-ME!"

Blaze shuddered. No one moved.

"Cre -**eeee** - **eeepy!"** sang Sugar out of the corner of her mouth.

"Agreed!" I hissed. "So, what do we do?"

"I don't <u>know!</u>" whispered Hannah.

The nearest teddy pricked up its ears.

"NO?" it echoed.

"NO?" questioned another.

The word 'NO' rippled through the bears.

Uh-oh!

They thought Hannah had said NO. They thought she'd refused to marry them.

Surely that couldn't end well?

The bear closest to Hannah shook his fluffy heart in outrage.

"MARRY ME!!!" he screamed.

"MARRY ME!" screamed the rest in reply.

And then they all **CHARGED.**

"Run!" squealed Hannah.

CHAPTER NINE

We ran!

The teddies were right on our heels, screaming at us to marry them.

"Over there! LOOK!" I yelled, pointing to a gate in a tall pink wall.

We **DIVED** through just in time and Blaze rammed the gate shut behind us, clanging a heavy metal bolt into place.

The teddies slammed into the metal bars, snarling with rage. Some of them tried to lift the bolt but it turned out their paws were stitched to the hearts they held which made it impossible for them to work the gate.

We were safe! For now at least!

And even better, it looked like we'd finally made it to Valentine's garden.

"Over there!" hissed Blaze, pointing

Sure enough, a dazzlingly handsome man was sitting at a large wooden desk. He was scribbling his way through a pile of pink cards.

Next to him was a stone Cupid, looking much happier than the guy we'd met, bubbling water into a pond.

"My love for you is like a dove..." murmured Valentine as he wrote, "...cheeky and likely to poop on your chocolates!"

He nodded happily.

"Oh yes, that's a good one!" he smiled.

He squirted the card with perfume and slid it into an envelope.

"Hello Mr Valentine," called Hannah marching over as if he might be expecting her.

Valentine was absolutely NOT expecting her. He was not expecting anyone!

In fact he was so surprised that he leapt about three metres into the air, knocking over cards and splashing perfume onto a passing sparrow.

The bird immediately got a dreamy expression and flew over to Blaze making kissing noises.

"Ohhhhhhhh," wailed Blaze, swatting the bird away. "Make it stop!"

"Never mind that!" Valentine spluttered. "How did you get past Cupid...and my petal monster...and the crazy marry-me bears?"

"Problem solving," I shrugged.

"And kindness," added Hannah.

"**And award-winning muuuusical taleeeeeeent!**" finished Sugar with a smug wink.

"Hmmph! I see," scowled Valentine, looking very unimpressed. "Well, go away! I don't like visitors."

Valentine went back to his letters.

The sparrow had flown off briefly but now it was back. It had pecked a 'marry me' heart from one of the teddies at the gate and now it was chasing Blaze round the garden with it.

"**No thank you-oooo!**" Blaze wailed. "**I don't want to marry you!**"

Meanwhile, back at the desk, Hannah was getting cross.

"Mr Valentine we are here because there is a serious problem at our school," she insisted with her hands on her hips.

"**A luuuurve problem**," added Sugar.

Valentine paused.

"Hmmmm. That <u>is</u> my favourite kind of problem," he admitted, looking up.

"You see, we were making heart man cards for Valentine's Day," I explained quickly, "and my teacher threw her card into the bin."

"She threw her card in the bin!" gasped Valentine, horrified. "I thought teachers were supposed to be smart. Your teacher must be dafter than a box of frogs."

"She isn't," said Hannah crossly. "Miss Green is very smart."

Valentine shrugged.

"If you say so. But Valentine's Day cards

can be very...ahhh...sensitive. He won't have liked being chucked in a bin!"

"No, he didn't," I agreed. "He's using his magic..."

"...**your love magic**..." accused Sugar, pointing at Valentine.

"to make people fall in love..." I finished.

"Great!" cried Valentine.

"...with the wrong people!" added Hannah.

"Ahhhhh," Valentine frowned. "Not so great."

"They're falling in love with people that don't love them back," explained Hannah. "He's trying to hurt everyone!"

"**And also there's this whole, snot petals and farty parties thing**," sang Sugar, grinning.

Meanwhile, the sparrow had ditched his heart cushion. Instead he was tugging a table towards Blaze. A table with a candlelit dinner for two!

"Oh noooooooooooooo," wailed Blaze.

It looked like worms were on the menu.

Valentine looked between Hannah and me thoughtfully.

"Hmmm," he said. "Only one solution for a card that's gone dotty as a Dalmatian. You'll need a magical gift."

Blaze nodded enthusiastically.

"Yes, please, Mr Valentine, Sir," he agreed before shouting. "And then we'll be leaving **AND NEVER COMING BACK. So I'm not**

really looking for a relationship!"

He glared pointedly at the sparrow but it just made more kissing noises and tried to tempt him to the table by wiggling the worms playfully.

"**Hmmmmmmm,**" said Valentine again stroking his chin. "**Okay then...**"

He pulled open a drawer in his desk and began to rummage through the contents.

"**Magical marriage teddy?**" he wondered, holding up a teddy like the ones at the gate. "**No. No. Not for this!**"

He tossed the teddy over his shoulder. It snarled and ran off. Valentine kept rooting around in his drawer.

"**Poisoned Perfume?**" he muttered. "**Hmm, maybe not around lots of children! Although, who would miss a few really... Ah-ha! This might work.**"

He pulled out a red, felted ring box and handed it to Hannah.

"There you go," he said proudly. "An enchanted ring box."

"Erm...We were hoping for something more like a weapon," said Hannah, looking doubtful. "Like some enchanted scissors maybe?"

"**Or an enchanted envelope,**" sang Sugar, smiling sweetly. "**Then we could post the heart-card baaaack to yoooooooooou.**"

"Don't you dare!" warned Valentine, shooting Sugar a dangerous look. "No, the ring box is what you need. Oh yes, and for the magic to work, that naughty card will need to open the ring box himself."

"**And how exaaaaaactly do we get him to do thaaaaat?**" sang Sugar.

Valentine shrugged.

"I'm sure you'll think of something..." he

wafted a hand towards me. "...problem solving and all that rubbish you said before. Now BOG OFF! I have cards to write."

"But," squeaked Blaze, "I...erm...HELP!"

Valentine looked around crossly and spotted Blaze. His sparrow friend had gone back to chasing him. And now it was dressed in a white wedding dress with a veil!

"You too!" snapped Valentine, flicking a finger towards them. "Go away!"

The sparrow's dreamy expression disappeared. It realised it was chasing a fire breathing dragon...

"TWEEET!!!" it screamed, flying off at top speed.

Behind us at the desk Valentine made an impatient noise.

"Urgh, why are you bothersome blobs still here?! People are so much noisier than letters!"

He snatched up an envelope, scribbled something on the front and then he screwed it up into a tight ball.

"Get your big, fat bums out of my garden NOW!" he yelled, hurling the envelope in our direction. It smacked Blaze on the side of the head but instead of bouncing off, the letter exploded into a cloud of pink smoke.

For a second I got this strange dreamy feeling. I felt like people were great and I should definitely hug them and maybe even feed them worms by candlelight.

But then the smoke cleared and we were magically back at school in the hall.

And things were looking bad!

Really, really bad!

CHAPTER TEN

The hall was in chaos.

Miss Green was chasing Mr Harding round the hall, blowing kisses. He was chasing Mrs Broom, who was violently sneezing petals, and she was chasing Mr Piddlestix.

Mr Piddlestix was screaming at the top of his voice, leaping over tables to escape and leaving a trail of fart roses wherever he went.

"Prince Charm-Bin! You came back!" sang Sugar, rushing over to a new bin and pulling it into a hug. **"Oh I missed you so much!"**

Her skin had turned that nasty neon pink again.

Hannah was clearly not impressed by this turn of events. In fact she looked furious.

"What's the plan?" she asked coldly.

"We need to keep Sugar and the teachers safe and out of the way," I said. "Blaze, you stay here and try to keep them all in the hall if you can."

"Use Sugar's technique and clunk 'em round the head with a pan if you have to!" added Hannah grimly.

"Okay," nodded Blaze turning his palest blue. "What about you?"

"We'll find the card!" I said frowning. "And then somehow get him to open the ring box."

"Come on," said Hannah, tugging me across the hall. "With so many of the teachers out of the way, he's probably back on that photocopier."

Unfortunately, she was right.

As we burst into the staff room, Hannah gasped. Card-Men covered every centimetre of the

floor. They perched on chairs and peered out from cupboards.

He'd made an army. And he was still making more copies!

"Get away from that photocopier," I called out as bravely as I could.

"Come to stop me, have you?" he sneered. "Well, as you can see, you're too late! Heeee heeee heeee!"

He waved his bendy paper arms around the room.

"Soon these cards will bounce off to post themselves," he boasted. "By tomorrow morning thousands of people will be in love..."

His eyes were shining with madness.

"...with toilets and cucumbers and who knows what else?" he finished, gleefully. "Heeee heee heee!"

He really was a lunatic!

I glanced at Hannah to see if she'd got any idea what we should do next, but Hannah was walking towards the Heart-Card-Man... looking dreamy.

"You're beautiful!" she murmured.

"Hannah?" I frowned. "What are you doing?"

Hannah ignored me, walking closer to the Heart-Card-Man.

"I. . . I love you," whispered Hannah, dreamily.

Heart-Card-Man looked puzzled but then his eyes widened in delight.

"Oh, I seeeeee!" he grinned wickedly. "Come here, little girl. Heeee heee"

"No!" I gasped. "Hannah! No!"

I tried to pull her back but she shrugged me off. And when I tried again she shoved me roughly to the floor. My own sister!

"Seize her!" yelled Heart-Card-Man, pointing at me and the card army rushed to do it, pinning me to the floor with their bendy card arms.

The magic had made them incredibly strong.

Hannah was almost to the card now.

"I love you so so much," she whispered passionately and she dropped to one knee holding out the magical ring box. "Will you... will you marry me?"

Suddenly it all made sense!

Hannah wasn't in love at all! It was just a trick!

In that moment, time seemed to stand still and all I could think was, *"Wow! Hannah's acting skills are crazy good. She really should be on TV!"*

Then Heart-Card-Man screamed in delight.

"Seriously? You're asking me to marry you?"

Hannah smiled and nodded.

Heart-Card-Man jumped down from the photocopier and bounced forward.

"Is that...a ring box?" he asked, excitedly.

Hannah nodded again, holding it out towards him and I held my breath.

He took the closed box gingerly.

"Take a look inside," urged Hannah.

The Heart-Card-Man gave an ugly, smug smile ... and then opened the box...

CHAPTER ELEVEN

There was an explosion of pink confetti. The card gasped and then clapped his papery hands in delight as the pink petals fluttered to the floor around him.

In the ring box lay a stunning diamond ring. It was a real whopper of a diamond but how would that help us?

Then I noticed something else.

The box was quivering in the card's hands, as if it was coming to life. And around the edges of the ring box were two rows of spiky, diamond teeth. In fact, the open box looked a lot like the gaping, hungry mouth of a piranha.

RAAAAR!

In a flash the ring box snarled into action, snapping its diamond teeth down hard onto one of the card's hands.

"EeeeeeeeeeeeeeK!" he squealed with a noise like a startled pig. "What? What is this?"

He shook his arm furiously trying to break free.

"OOOOOOOUCHIEOUCHIE OUCH!"

he whimpered. "Get it off! Get it off!"

The other cards rushed to help. Even the ones that were meant to be holding me.

I was free.

The card army tugged and heaved, trying to prise open the ring box jaws. But it was clamped on to Heart-Card-Man's hand like a crocodile and it wasn't about let go.

"Eeeeeeeeeeeeek! Do something!" he yelled.

The cards scrambled over one another to help, pushing and pulling until...

RIIIIIIIP!

"Eeeeeeeeeeeeeeeeeek!" screeched Heart-Card Man. "My arm! My arm's been ripped clear off! Oh, I think I'm gonna be sick!"

The card army stumbled back from their leader in horror. He was free...**but his arm was no longer stuck to his heart shaped body...**

...IT WAS DANGLING FROM THE JAWS OF THE RING BOX!

And it looked like the ring box wasn't done yet!

In the blink of an eye, it **SHOT** towards the card again and bit off his pointed papery bum.

"Eeeeeeeeeeeek!" screamed Heart-Card-Man, leaping into the air in pain.

When he hit the ground he was only an M shape with one bendy arm.

"The ring box!" he gasped to his army, bouncing away and pointing towards the box with his one remaining arm. "Kill the ring box!"

But before a single card could move, either to attack or (more likely) hide, the ring box turned to consider the card army with a low growl.

Then, with a snarl of rage, it **ZIPPED** into the crowd of paper, **TEARING AND SHREDDING,**

destroying everything in its path!

"Nooooooo!" screamed Heart-Card-Man. "That's my army! Nooooooooooooooooooo!"

The ring box was **ZOOMING** round the floor now like a remote control robot, **CHOMPING** every papery thing it could find.

A few of the smarter cards started trying to hide which seemed like our cue to help.

"Come on!" yelled Hannah, obviously thinking the same thing.

We **DASHED** round the room, yanking cards out of their hiding spots and tossing them into the path of the ring box that **WHIZZED** round the floor.

CHOMP went the diamond teeth...

CHOMP...

CHOMP...

CHOMP!

Until there was just one card left...
The card that had started it all!

As the room fell suddenly silent, what was left of Heart-Card-Man appeared on top of the photocopier once more. He was propping himself up on his one remaining bendy arm.

"Enough! Pleeeease!" he whimpered. "I just wanted to be loved! Is that a crime?"

Across the room I saw Hannah's face crumple in sympathy.

"Well, of course not," she started to say kindly, "You just need..."

She never got time to finish.

Heart-Card-Man SPRANG towards her...

an evil gleam in his eye...

a teacher's staple gun in his hand!

"NOOOO!" I screamed, RUNNING AND

LEAPING in front of Hannah. But something else was leaping too.

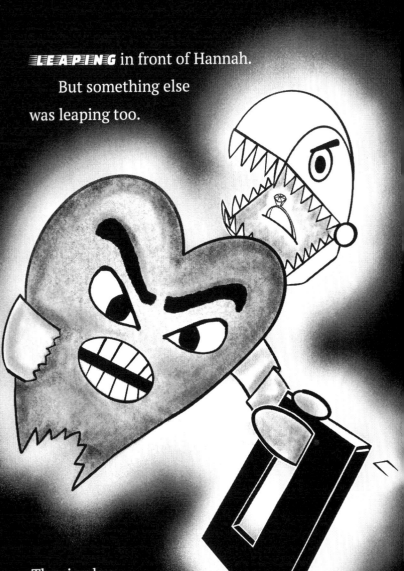

The ring box **SPRANG** from the floor, **colliding** in mid air with Heart-Card-Man and **clamping** to what remained of his body.

"Eeeeeeeeeeeeeeeeeeeeeeeek" he screeched.

But that was all he had time to say.

With a **BUZZ** of **SUPER FAST CHOMPING** those diamond teeth **SHREDDED** the last bits of Heart-Card-Man into a cloud of confetti and the staple gun fell to the floor with a **THUMP**.

The ring box landed next to it and **SPUN FROM SIDE TO SIDE** as if searching for any further trouble.

But every last card was in pieces.

Satisfied, the ring box blew a **huge raspberry of confetti**, transformed back into a boring and perfectly ordinary ring box, snapped shut and lay silent.

"Well," squeaked Hannah eventually. "That was close!"

I nodded. I wasn't sure I could even speak just yet.

Hannah hung her head and her shoulders slumped.

"I really thought he was sorry," she whispered sadly. "I guess I was being a bit stupid."

"Giving second chances isn't stupid," I said firmly. "It's kind. Just, in future, maybe be kind from... you know, a bit further away..."

We looked at each other, considering this. Then we both started to giggle.

At that moment Blaze peeked his head around the door.

"Is he gone?" he whispered.

"Yep!" nodded Hannah. "The ring box shredded him to bits. And all his friends."

She gestured round the room at the mountains of confetti.

"Woah!" said Blaze, taking in the scene.

The staff room really needed a hoover!

Sugar blasted in over Blaze's head and did a joyful loop the loop. Her skin was changing colour from it's normal purple shade to a happy golden yellow.

"**Wooo hoooo!**" she sang giving one of the confetti piles a joyful kick. "**Cut into bits, and you're to blame, you give lo-o-ove, a bad name!**"

"Oh Sugar!" giggled Hannah. "It's good to have you back!"

CHAPTER TWELVE

Everything was back to normal.

Except that we'd been called down to the hall for an end of day assembly. I had to admit that

was a bit odd for a Wednesday.

Blaze was hiding inside my school jumper just

in case there was a new magical problem that needed fixing.

"What did Sugar do with the ring box?" I hissed, as we walked down the corridor.

"She left it on Mr Harding's desk," he whispered. "With a note saying that he'd won it in a competition."

"Surely he wont believe that?" I murmured into my jumper. "People don't just **win** diamond rings. **That's ridiculous!**"

Dear Mr Harding,

CONGRATULATIONS!

You have won first prize in Valentine's RING Competition!

You may not remember entering, but you definitely did.

Love and hugs,
St Valentine

"You'd be amazed what people will and won't believe," Blaze chuckled.

As we sat down in our class lines I could see Hannah across the hall. She tapped a Sugar shaped bulge in her cardigan and gave me a wink.

Meanwhile, at the front of the hall Mrs Broom

had started talking.

"...and Mr Piddlestix has made you all some chocolate to take home for Valentine's Day."

Everyone cheered, especially me and Hannah.

(I figured we deserved a truck load of chocolates after the day we'd just had!)

"Although," continued Mrs Broom. "He will be sticking to his ordinary job from now on, won't you Mr Piddlestix."

"Yes," he agreed looking his usual grumpy self.

The love magic had definitely worn off for those two!

"Now Mr Harding," said Mrs Broom. "Time for your bit! And Miss Green, you'd best come up too, in case he **needs a hand**."

For some reason, Mrs Broom chuckled to herself as if she'd just made a great joke.

"What now?" I hissed to Blaze, feeling uneasy.

"I bet I can guess," he hissed back.

When the two teachers got to the front, Mr

Harding pulled out the red ring box (minus razor teeth) and dropped onto one knee.

Everyone gasped.

Miss Green looked stunned and at the side Mrs Broom gave an excited little clap.

"Miss Green...Sophie," smiled Mr Harding. "Will you marry me?"

WHAT!?!?

From across the hall Hannah gave me a thumbs up and a look like 'See, I told you so'.

"This isn't more crazy love magic, is it?" I asked Blaze, just to be sure.

"No," he whispered, peeking out of my jumper towards the teachers. "This is the real thing...but still quite magical."

Whatever!

As long as no one was hugging a bin, I was happy.

Miss Green had started to cry and laugh at the same time.

"Yes!" she said. "Yes! Yes!"

Mr Harding pushed the diamond ring on to

her finger and then leapt up to give her a smoochy kiss.

Everyone cheered. Except Ben of course who pretended to be sick on the floor. (He really is just that sort of boy.)

"Yes, well," grinned Mrs Broom breaking it up. "That's quite enough of the mushy love stuff for one day!"

I couldn't agree more!

Who would YOU draw farting petals?

How did the telephone propose to the teacher?

It gave them a ring!

Quiz: Which character are you?

1. You are making a sandcastle at the seaside when a football smashes it down. Do you:

a) Decide evil birds kicked the football and run into the sea (fully clothed) chasing a confused looking seagull.

b) Write a sad song about a football that broke the heart of a castle.

c) Ask the football to marry you.

2. Your Great Granny's 100th birthday cake unexpectedly explodes. Do you:

a) Search the icing for telltale feathers – those evil birds did it!

b) Keep on singing Happy Birthday and hope your Great Granny doesn't notice.

c) Ask your Great Granny to marry you.

3. Your baby sister does an incredibly smelly poo in her nappy. Do you:

a) Decide your baby sister is actually a robotic

pooing machine operated by birds.

b) Cover the nappy in petals to get rid of the smell.

c) Ask the nappy to marry you.

4. You're in the toilet when you realise there is no toilet roll left. Do you:

a) Decide birds must have stolen it all. Then find one last roll but throw it out of the window at a passing sparrow.

b) Stay in the toilet forever just writing cool songs and chilling out.

c) Ask the toilet to marry you.

If answered mostly A, you're Cupid. Mostly B, you're Petal. Mostly C, you're one of the Marry-Me bears.

(If you're most like Cupid you really should calm down, get yourself a pet parrot with laser eyes and learn to love birds.)

Go to <u>www.jennyyork.com</u> for lots more FUN!

R	A	A	E	I	E	D	A	G	G	A	E	V	T
R	B	L	A	Z	E	L	R	H	C	I	T	T	Z
U	T	S	E	P	L	Z	D	B	I	L	H	A	M
A	V	D	M	L	C	I	D	P	A	E	R	Z	E
C	A	R	D	N	P	O	U	B	D	R	E	T	D
N	L	N	U	U	C	U	I	G	G	A	C	A	R
N	E	E	C	A	E	A	A	L	U	G	R	E	E
I	N	I	C	H	D	R	A	G	U	S	S	V	I
B	T	R	A	E	H	T	Z	L	R	I	O	E	I
M	I	N	I	N	E	E	I	L	C	L	S	M	C
R	N	R	G	P	M	R	S	Z	V	M	A	A	L
A	E	I	A	R	P	T	G	P	H	R	G	G	A
H	A	N	E	X	I	T	S	E	L	D	D	I	P
C	A	G	D	E	I	A	R	E	A	L	A	C	T

CHARMBIN   CARD

RING   PIDDLESTIX

MAGIC   PETAL

LOVE   VALENTINE

SUGAR   BLAZE

HEART   CUPID

Go to www.jennyyork.com for lots more FUN!

Look out for:

Printed in Great Britain
by Amazon

75864627R00066